In the Nick of Time

Bill Myers and Robert West

Based on characters created by Bill Myers and Ken C. Johnson; the story by George Taweel and Rob Loos; and the teleplay by Martha Williamson.

Tyndale House Publishers, Inc.
Wheaton, Illinois

For Larry, Julie, Amy, Erin, and Philip

Library of Congress Cataloging-in-Publication Data

Myers, Bill, date
In the nick of time / Bill Myers and Robert West.
p. cm.
"Focus on Family presents: McGee and me!"
"Based on characters created by Bill Myers and Ken C. Johnson, the story by George Taweel and Rob Loos, and the teleplay by Martha Williamson."
Summary: While mountain climbing with his father and friends in California, seventh grader Nick calls on God to help him deal with various fears and dangers.
ISBN 0-8423-4122-6
[1. Mountaineering—Fiction. 2. Christian life—Fiction.]
I. West, Robert, date. II. Title.
PZ7.M98234In 1993
[Fic]—dc20 93-16107

Printed in the United States of America

98 97 96 95 94 93
7 6 5 4 3 2

Contents

"Don't be afraid, for the Lord will go before you and will be with you; he will not fail nor forsake you." (Deuteronomy 31:8, *The Living Bible*)

ONE
Beginnings

"Ladies and gentlemen," the announcer shouted over the arena's PA system. "Guys and gals, babes and babettes—despite popular demand, untold bribes, and threats from every civilized leader in every civilized country of our civilized world (as well as Toledo) . . ."

The audience grew silent in anticipation.

"It is my reluctant pleasure to announce that . . ."

A drum began to roll.

"McGEE IS BACK!"

The crowd went wild. Literally. I could hear them breaking windows, tearing up seats, lighting flame-throwers—anything to prevent me from coming on stage. But, as luck would have it, there were only eighty thousand of them. And a mob of eighty thousand is no match for someone with my egotistically egocentric ego.

The curtain parted and there I was: McGee the Magnificent, world-famous magician and part-time encyclopedia salesman.

"Throw him off the stage! Get rid of the bum!" a woman screamed.

"C'mon, Mom, be reasonable . . . ," I said to her, but soon the entire arena picked up the chant.

I couldn't blame them. Ever since I had said the magic words and accidentally transformed all the world's hamburgers into broccoliburgers people had been a little touchy. Something about driving through the Golden Arches and asking for a Big Broc didn't set well. They weren't crazy about the side orders of French fried asparagus or the cream of cauliflower shakes, either. OK, so they weren't very tasty. But hey, they were healthy.

Even so, this was no time to gloat over past accomplishments. I had to do what I had to do, so I did it! Quicker than you can say, "How many pages does this go on before we get to the real story?" I had wheeled my magic trunk onto the stage.

I took my trusty magic wand (which really isn't magic cause there is no such thing as magic, only tricks and optical illusions . . . well, except for those broccoliburgers. . . .) Anyway, I took my trusty optical-illusion wand, waved it over the trunk, and said the magic—er, optical-illusion words:

"Abracadabra,
Laurel and Stan,
Walla Walla Washington,
Bam! Bam! Bam!"

Suddenly, the trunk lid flew open and out popped the sinister dental assistant, Nurse Nerveless. In her hand was a beaker containing the Secret Sour Formula—the formula that had changed all the world's sweetness to sourness in one of my earlier fantasies.

"Nurse Nerveless!" I shouted. "What are you doing here?"

She looked around, confused. "Isn't this Book Five?"

"No, no, no! This is Book Ten," I explained.

"Oh, so sorry," she said as she climbed back into the trunk.

"Don't worry, even I get them confused," I said while closing the lid on her. "See you around."

She nodded and, in a puff of imagination, was replaced by the dreaded and dastardly . . . Designer Dude.

The crowd gasped.

"Put him back, put him back! Not Designer Dude!" they screamed. But it was too late. He was already out of the trunk and criticizing them for what they wore.

"Is that a dress, sweetheart?" he called to someone in the first row. "Or did the sports store have a sale on tents?"

The woman looked around in embarrassment, then darted for the exit.

"I don't want to say those pants are out of style, mister," he shouted to another person, "but check to see if they're made out of fig leaves and have Adam's name sewn on the inside."

Soon he had the entire crowd racing for the doors in embarrassment. Then he turned his dastardly designer digs upon me.

I swallowed hard. Having worn the same blue jeans, red sweatshirt, and adorably cute yellow suspenders in every book, I knew this could get messy. But I also knew I was the hero of these little stories, and heroes always win. I raised my magic wand—but, alas and alack, he was too quick.

"Hey, McGee! Are those tennis shoes, or did you forget to take off your water skis?"

The blow knocked me to my knees. Hey, it wasn't my fault Nicholas drew me with size fifteen feet. It was time to fight fire with fire . . . or at least bad jokes with bad jokes. I pulled out my wand and started waving it and shouting:

"Ophra and Donahue,
Aresenio and Jay.
You're now dressed like the Brady Bunch,
Look down and be crazed!"

Suddenly Designer Dude was wearing clothes from the 70s! That's right. Bell-bottom pants, platform shoes, a super-wide belt, and a flower-print shirt with the peace sign on the back! To top it off, everything was made of polyester!

"AUGHHHH! Get it off me!" he screamed. "Get it off! Get it off!"

I blew the smoke from the barrel of my trusty wand, twirled it around, and dropped it neatly into my holster. "Sorry, Designer," I drawled in my best John Wayne imitation, "but I think ya better be headin' outta town."

"But-but where . . . where could I possibly go

wearing this . . . this . . ." He could barely get out the word, "this . . . polyester?"

"Well," I offered, "there's always Christian TV talk shows."

Before Designer could gasp I heard another voice.

"McGee, what are you doing?"

Suddenly Designer Dude vanished, along with the arena and everything else. Well, everything else but my trunk. Now I was standing on the Martins' kitchen counter, and my good buddy and creator Nicholas Martin was looking down at me.

"You're supposed to be packing for our vacation," he said as he reached for a nearby bag of chips.

"Yeah," I shot back, "but it would sure help if I knew where I was packing for."

Nicky boy sighed in agreement and glanced over to the party going on in the family room. Everybody was there—fashion queen Renee and her mom, Prince of the wimps Philip and his dad, and, of course, the obligatory big sister Sarah and little sister Jamie. It was a swell Bon-Voyage party. The only problem was that Mom and Dad weren't telling Nick where we were Bon Voyaging to!

"Still no word?" I asked.

"Not a peep," Nick said as he opened the fridge for some more dip.

Immediately my imaginative imagination began to imagine. "I've got it!" I shouted as I whipped out the canoe and paddle I always keep handy for just such occasions. "We're gonna canoe down the Amazon!"

Nick shook his head.

I tossed the canoe and paddle into the trunk.

Next I pulled out hip boots, a pith helmet, and a neck-load of cameras. "Trekking across the African Wilds?"

Nick gave a shrug. "Who knows, but if they've all cooked up this 'Big Surprise Vacation,' then it's gotta be pretty big, right?"

"You don't mean . . . ," I gasped in breathless anticipation, "not the . . . the Tulip Festival of Michigan!"

Nick gave me one of his sarcastic looks. I gotta hand it to the kid, it was pretty sarcastic. He'd been practicing. I guess that's one of the advantages of having two sisters bugging you all the time. You get lots of practice.

"Why all the hush-hush?" I asked as I tried to cram my favorite surfboard and some scuba gear into the trunk. I would have taken my twenty-foot bass boat and my monster dirt bike along, too, but I like to pack light.

Nick just shrugged. He plopped a chip into his mouth and headed back to the family room. He'd managed to get a dab of dip on the end of his nose. I was going to warn him, but since everyone was being so secretive I figured I'd have a little secret of my own.

I turned back to the trunk and—Arrrrgh! Rrrrrrumph! Gruhhhhhh!—tried to shut the lid. "UUUUmmmmph!" There. Now it's just a matter of closing this little latch here and . . .

S P R O I N G ! !

The tin-plated, overgrown jack-in-the-box flung me halfway to Kokomo . . . well, at least to the other end of the counter, where I decided to just lay quietly for a while—at least until someone came along to dig me out from under my two-ton pile of stuff.

Still wearing the chip dip, Nick headed out of the kitchen to join Renee and Philip.

"Look," Philip giggled, "it's Rudolph the Onion-Dip–Nosed Reindeer."

Nick reached up and wiped the white goo away as quickly as possible. He liked a good joke as much as the next guy. He just wasn't crazy about *being* the joke.

Philip's dad rose from the nearby couch and crossed to join Nick's mom at the bowl of chips. He was the type of guy you'd expect to see on those TV sitcoms—you know, the big goofy next-door neighbor who always came over and did big goofy things? "Big Phil," as they called him, was a dentist. That meant he had to stay away from sugar (it's like a law or something), but every other food seemed fair game.

So far he'd demolished twenty-seven trays of chips, veggies, and dip. At the moment he was going for number twenty-eight.

"Great chips, Liz," he said a little too loudly—he always said things a little too loudly—as he took the bowl of the goodies from her hands and dumped them onto his plate.

Nick's mom forced a polite smile. When it came to Big Phil, she had polite smiling down to a science.

"Gotta build up my strength," he said with a crunch while motioning toward the kids. "I'm gonna need all my stamina to spend a whole week with three teenagers having fun doing you-know-what . . . you-know-where!"

"My, when you keep a secret, you really keep a secret, don't you?" Mom said, trying to laugh along. She should have won an Oscar for her performance. Or a pair of ear plugs. Not only did Big Phil talk loud, he laughed loud. Louder than loud. Scrunch-your-face-in-pain loud.

"Ha! Ha! Liz, that's a good one! A dandy! Ha!"

The louder Big Phil laughed, the glummer his son became. "My dad's too happy," the boy mumbled, watching his father. "We must be going to a dentist's convention."

"That sounds awful," Renee groaned.

"I'll say," Philip agreed. "No sweets, and mandatory flossing between events."

Nick refused to give up hope. He was sure Philip was wrong. "I saw my dad pack a swimsuit, so it must be some place with a pool."

"Dentists swim, too, you know," Philip replied.

"It's gotta be California," Renee insisted. "That's where we're going."

"How do you know?" Philip asked.

Renee explained. "Wherever we're going, my dad's going to join us, right? And he lives in California, right? And he's been wanting me to visit, so it all makes sense. Right?"

"Wrong," Philip sighed, looking even glummer. "That's the same kind of logic they use to prove Elvis is still alive."

Nicholas glanced up to the computer-generated banner draped across the wall. Bon Voyage, it said. He had no idea what "bon" meant, but the closer they got to the "voyage," the weirder everything about this vacation got.

Weird Point One: Neither Mom nor Nick's sisters were going on the trip. Nick didn't mind leaving his sisters behind. It would be good to have a little peace and quiet for a change. But why not Mom? Sure, Grandma was coming home from the hospital next week and Mom needed to take care of her. But they could have rescheduled the vacation, couldn't they?

Weird Point Two: Philip and Renee *were* going. They were OK, of course, on a once-in-a-decade basis, but . . . for a whole week? What were he and Philip supposed to talk about? Algebra? What were the guys at school gonna think when they found out that he went on vacation with Philip, the all-school brain, and Renee, the . . . the . . . *girl!?* Oh sure, Nick had started to realize that girls weren't as gross as he thought (except, of course, for his sisters, who were getting grosser all the time!). Even so, who wanted to go on vacation with one?

No doubt about it, this secret vacation was gonna have to *stay secret.*

While the three kids sat on the back of the couch gloomily considering their fate, little sister Jamie crawled up onto her dad's lap. "Daddy," she whined, dropping cheese-puff crumbs from her mouth with every word. "Why can't I go, too?"

"Maybe in a few years," Dad said as he gently brushed the bright orange crumbs off his pants. "But this trip is for me and your brother. We need to spend some time together. You know, to learn about each other."

"You don't need a vacation for *that,*" Jamie quipped. "Trust me, I can tell you *all* you'll ever want to know about Nick." With that she swiveled off of Dad's lap and strutted past her brother, her tongue stuck out.

Nicholas lifted his arms in befuddlement. "What'd I do?" Then it dawned on him. In a few years Jamie would also be a teenager—just like big sister Sarah. Not only a teenager, but a *girl* teenager. Of course. That explained it. That explained it all. "Like sister, like sister," he said with a sigh.

"Dad!" he complained as his father wiped off the last of the cheese crumbs. "When are you going to tell us where we're going?"

"Soon," he said as he rose and headed for the book shelf. "But I'll give you a hint." He pulled a Bible off of the shelf and flipped through the pages. "Ah, here it is." He began reading aloud: "'God fills me with strength and protects me wherever I go. He gives me the surefootedness of a mountain goat upon the crags.'"

"We're going to the zoo?" Nick asked, smirking.

Dad gave him one of his famous "Dad Looks."

Sarah returned from the kitchen carrying a sheet cake. "Here's another hint," she said with a nod to the writing on the cake.

The kids gathered around. Philip cocked his head and read: "'Happy Trails'?"

"Oh, brother! Another riddle," Nick moaned. "This is torture."

Meanwhile Big Phil was letting go of another one of his obnoxious laughs. "Oooh, what a beautiful cake!"

Mom proudly nodded to her daughter. "Sarah made it all by herself."

"Mom!" Sarah rolled her eyes in embarrassment. "I've been making cakes for five years."

"Yeah," Jamie chimed in, "but we've only been able to eat them for two years."

Nicholas looked at Jamie with surprised admiration. *Not bad for a nine-year-old,* he thought. *Maybe I can make an ally out of her yet. A few pointers here, some lessons in brotherly respect there, and—*

"OK, attention everyone!"

Nick glanced up to see Dad holding up a can of soda. "The time has finally come for us dad types to reveal our surprise destination. Drum roll, please."

Everyone obliged. Some on the table. Others on the back of chairs. Others with their mouths. Actually it was pretty pathetic. But, then again, the Martins had never claimed to be musical.

"Nick, Philip, and Renee," Dad said with a flourish. "Pack your bags and get ready for the time of your life! It's . . . *California, here we come!*"

"Yes!" Renee screamed. "I knew it! Next stop: Beverly Hills!"

"Wow!" Philip cried, already having visions of movie lots and bright lights. "I wonder if we'll meet any movie stars?"

Dad lifted his can higher in a toast. "To our courageous kids, Nick and Philip and Renee. . . ."

"Courageous?" Philip squeaked. Suddenly he wasn't quite as enthusiastic. What did being courageous have to do with a dream vacation in California?

Dad Martin continued. "May we return from this adventure stronger and wiser and closer . . ."

"Adventure?" It was Renee's turn to worry. "I don't want adventure. I want sun and sand and Christian Slater!"

In spite of the noticeable mood shift, Dad Martin kept right with his toast: ". . . having grown and stretched ourselves, and met this thrilling and exciting challenge."

"Stretched? Challenge?" Now all three kids groaned. The words were wrong. All wrong. Fun, yes. Adventure . . . maybe. But courage? Strength? *Stretching?* What was going on?

They were about to find out.

TWO

Toto, We're Not in Indiana Anymore

"Mountain climbing?" Nicholas gasped for the three hundredth time since Dad had announced the vacation. And for the three hundredth time he hoped it was just a bad dream. But as Nick looked around him, he couldn't deny the truth any longer. This bad dream was for real.

Philip, Renee, and Nick had just unloaded their backpacks from the station wagon. Now, three time zones and half a continent away from home, they stood on a cliff overlooking mountains and valleys.

"It's definitely *not* Beverly Hills," Philip moaned.

Renee nodded. "How far do you think it is to the nearest video store?"

Yes sir, there was nothing like the great outdoors to make you appreciate the finer things in life: CDs . . . big-screen TVs . . . flushing toilets. No such luxuries here. This was definitely life on the edge. Clint Eastwood territory. Survival of the fittest.

"So, just out of curiosity," Philip said while eyeing the mountains, "how long do you usually have to wear a body cast? Six, seven months?"

"You're not going to break anything," Renee said, plunking a hand on her cocked hip. She'd been doing a lot of that lately. Nick was sure it was only a matter of time before she plunked too hard and threw the whole hip out of joint.

"You're right," Philip answered as he stared at the cliffs, glassy-eyed. "I'll pass out first."

"C'mon, guys," Nick's dad called from the station wagon. "We've got lots of gear to sort out."

While the guys were sorting out their stuff I figured it was time to hop out of Nicky boy's sketch pad and hit the beach. Yes-siree-bob, I'd donned my Foster Grants and my Beach Boys Hawaiian shirt and was ready for some sand and fun and sun.

Imagine my shock and dismay when I couldn't find the ocean . . . or the the surf . . . or the babes . . . OR THE GROUND!? YIKES!! I wasn't at the ocean, I was standing on the edge of the world! And there was nothing but a whole lot of nothing in front of me. One false move and I'd be falling faster than a bad sitcom in the Nielson ratings.

Carefully, ever so cautiously, I inched my precious tootsies backward until I was safe and secure on the mountain cliff.

MOUNTAIN?

CLIFF??

Well, I guess that takes care of my surfing lessons. Hmmm, let's see, what does an incredibly handsome cartoon-type wear to scale the heights these days? I crossed over to my trunk, opened it, and started looking.

"Fireman's uniform . . . nah. Space suit . . . nope." Deeper and deeper I dug. Before I knew it I was in so deep I was hanging onto the edge of the trunk with my toes.

"Indian chief's headdress . . . Antarctica explorer suit . . . Diving bell . . . Nope, nada, nix. Ahhh, here we go. Purrrfecct."

I reached down for my Swiss yodeler's costume when suddenly my toes slipped. (That's the disadvantage of being a cartoon type and only having eight of 'em. Toes, that is.) I began falling. Farther and farther into the trunk I tumbled. Deeper and deeper I fell. Then, just when I was wondering if I had anything to wear while visiting China, I hit bottom.

K-THWANK!

I looked up. There was a tiny ray of light above me, but it was miles away.

I shouted, "Nicholas!" and the echo bounced all around me. "-olas-olas-olas!"

No answer.

"Can any body-ody-ody hear-ear me-me-me?"

Still no answer. Only this stupid echo-cho-cho. Hey wait a minute-inute-inute. It's not suppose to echo-cho-cho when I think-ink-ink. It's only suppose to echo-cho-cho when I talk-alk-alk-alk.

"Hey-ey-ey-ey!" I shouted-ed-ed-ed. "Will you knock it off-ff-ff with the echo-cho-cho-cho?"

No response.

"I said-aid-aid, will you knock it off with the echo?"

There. That's better. "Testing: one, two, three." No echo. Good. I wonder how they do that anyway.

Now where were we? Oh yeah. My situation was hopeless. Well, hopeless for normal mortals. But not for us mighty McGee types. No-siree-bob. Quicker than you can say, "Now what's he got up his sleeve?" I pulled a rocket jet pack out from—you guessed it—my sleeve.

I strapped the jet pack on, flipped the switch to "Let's-get-outta-here-and-fast!" and roared up and out of the trunk.

As McGee was finishing his adventures in trunk-land, Renee looked up from her packing. She spotted a man heading in their direction. He was trim, handsome, and fortyish. Oh, and one other thing. He was her father.

"Dad!" she cried and ran toward him at about warp nine. When she arrived she threw herself into his arms.

"Hi, sweetheart!" the man said as he held her tight. There was no missing the emotion in his voice. After a long moment he put her at arms' length for a better look, then pulled her back in for another hug, and then put her back out for another look. At this rate, Nick wondered if the poor girl would need orthopedic surgery before she got home.

"I hardly recognized you," her father said, his voice hoarse with emotion. "You've really grown." Before Renee could answer he pulled her in for another hug.

Dad Martin and Big Phil crossed toward them

from the station wagon. "Hey, Ted," Dad Martin said, "it's great to see you again."

Renee's father looked up and then rose to shake Dad Martin's hand. "It's great to see you, David. Hey, Phil, glad you could make it."

"Wouldn't miss it for the world," Big Phil bellowed. "Right, Son?" The big man grinned as he slapped a hand on Philip's shoulder. Philip did his best to grin back.

Just then a good-looking all-American type jogged out from under the trees. "Hi, everybody!" he called. Beside him, moving stride for stride, was a cool-looking, bright-eyed Latin woman.

"Welcome to Wilderness Adventures," the guy said as he approached. "I'm your senior guide, Brad Gifford, but you can call me Giff." Flashing Nick and the others an award-winning smile, Giff turned to his female companion. "This is my co-leader, Consuela—"

"Connie, for short," she interrupted with a dazzling grin of her own. Suddenly Nick thought things weren't going to be so bad after all. Now that he was entering seventh grade he was beginning to think of girls as something other than targets for spit wads. Let's face it, this lady was definitely not in the spit-wad category. Besides, she looked like she could outrun, outshoot, and outspit any of them.

Brad continued, "Connie and I will be your guides as the six of you make up what we call a 'Struggle Group'."

"He's got that right," Philip whispered to Nicholas.

Nick rolled his eyes in agreement. "Struggle group?" Couldn't they just watch it on TV? You know, a National Geographic documentary or something?

"In the next few days," Giff continued, "we'll be teaching you mountain climbing techniques, and you'll even learn some wilderness survival skills."

Now it was Renee's turn to roll her eyes. Teaching? Learning? *What's going on here?* Everybody knows that three months out of every year kids are expected to hang "No Vacancy" signs on their brains.

"And you can be sure that by the end of the week," Connie added, "each of you will have learned something about yourselves. The woods have a quiet way of exposing our fears. They also bring us closer to each other . . . and to God."

"Good thing," gulped Nicholas, looking at the cliffs. "I'm gonna need him."

"So," Giff concluded with an all-too-cheery voice, "we'll be ready to move just as soon as you pack our supplies into your packs."

"*Your* supplies into *our* packs?" Nicholas asked.

Giff and Connie exchanged amused looks. "It's not much, Nick . . . just a few odds and ends."

The kids turned in the direction he was pointing. Before them lay a small mountain of "odds and ends." With more than a few groans the kids dragged their packs over to the new gear and started packing.

Everyone but Philip. He just sort of stood over his pack, staring.

"What are you doing?" Nick asked.

"I'm confronting my fear," Philip answered.

Nicholas looked around, puzzled. "What fear?"

"My fear of being crushed under all this stuff."

Renee also had her share of problems. "How do I pack all this junk?" she whined as she stacked things in order. Organization was Renee's thing. Even in a food fight, she'd make sure the dessert was thrown last. "Heavy things first?" she asked. "How about . . . clothes on the bottom, food on the top?" She shook her head and switched the stacks around again. "Alphabetically? No, no, no. . . . Maybe . . ." She shook out the bag and suddenly—

"EEEEEK!" She jumped back as a three-foot snake fell to the ground! Everyone froze. Everyone but Big Phil. He raced to the snake, grabbed it by the neck, and started choking it. It was a fight to the death. Man vs. snake. Snake vs. man. What a guy. . . . What a hero. . . .

What a jokester.

Suddenly Big Phil burst out laughing. Everyone looked puzzled. The guy continued to laugh even louder. He was really cracking himself up. "I'm sorry," he finally gasped to Renee. "This was supposed to be in Philip's pack."

Philip stared at his dad, wide-eyed. "You put a snake in my pack?"

"A rubber snake," Big Phil said, laughing even louder as he wiggled it in front of their noses. "Just a little wilderness humor between father and son."

Everyone heaved a sigh of relief. Everyone but Philip. "This is going to be a long week," he sighed. "Actually, it's going to be a long *adolescence*."

THREE
Fear Appears

Speaking of "fear," Nick had some of his own. It had to do with the steep, narrow mountain trail they were hiking on; the steep, narrow mountain trail that kept getting steeper and steeper and narrower and narrower. Actually, it wasn't hiking *on* the trail that had him frightened, it was the fear of hiking *off* the trail. *Way* off—and straight down for about two thousand feet!

Dad Martin didn't notice anything was wrong with his son. He was too busy taking pictures. "Wow! Look at that!" *CLICK*. "Wow, look at this!" *CLICK*. Dad and his camera were having the time of their lives. It was here a "Wow! *CLICK*," there a "Wow! *CLICK*," everywhere a "Wow! *CLICK*."

The three stoogelings weren't so impressed. They could have seen this same stuff on PBS or the Discovery Channel every day of the week. So what was the big deal?

"Wow!" Dad called. "Check out the waterfall on that mountain over there!" *CLICK*.

Nick took a look across the valley. OK. It *was* incredible the way the water fell and fell, gradually turning to pure mist by the time it hit the valley floor. And then there was the giant rainbow the water formed! The colors were so sharp and pure it was like looking through a prism.

"I tell you, guys," Dad continued, "nobody does special effects better than God."

Maybe he's got a point, Nick thought, until a blue jay suddenly made a bombing run over his head.

SPLAT!

Then again, there are some special effects he could do without.

Farther up the trail, Renee and her father were talking. Actually it was more like her father was talking, and Renee was doing all the listening. (As far as Nick could tell, that was some kind of first for Renee.)

"You just have to remember, life's very different now," her dad explained.

"I know, Dad," Renee answered.

"You have to work harder in junior high."

"I know, Dad."

"You're starting to become an adult."

"I know, Dad." If Renee had been thinking, she would have recorded those three words on a tape loop and set her portable cassette deck on continuous replay.

"You have to choose your friends carefully."

"I know, Dad."

"This is pretty complicated stuff," he pointed out. "Maybe I should be writing it down.

"I don't think so, Dad. . . ."

A half hour later Giff led the group around the final bend. "Ta daaah!!" he sang as he motioned to the scenery. "This is it. When you go back to Indiana, you'll all be able to say that you climbed . . . ," he stepped aside so all could see. "THE GIANT!"

Soaring majestically into the sky was a huge, sheer rock face. If you tilted your head, squinted one eye, and let your imagination run a little amok, the formation did look something like the looming face of a giant.

"They've got to be kidding," Renee gasped.

"I can't climb that," Philip gulped. "I can't even *look* at that."

Nick didn't say a thing. Fear had grabbed him by the throat. You know, that slimy, hairy, ax-wielding, paralyzing blob that used to hide under our beds, but, now that we're older, just lurks in our minds? That's the emotion I'm talking about. Right then, it had Nick in its molars and was chomping down hard. In some foggy recess of his brain he heard Giff's final words: "Let's keep pushing on, we've got to make camp before nightfall."

Somehow Nick managed to move his feet, but you'd have thought his head was screwed on backward the way he trudged one direction and kept looking back over his shoulder at . . .

The Giant.

Nick was still worried that night as they set up camp and prepared to eat. But facing the Giant wasn't going to be his only fear.

"Make sure you hang your food packs high

enough in the trees so the bears won't get them," Giff explained as he scooped Philip's pack from the ground and hung it on a nearby branch.

"What about me?" Philip squeaked. "*I'm* sleeping on the ground."

The group chuckled, but Philip didn't join in. He was too busy glancing around for his own tree branch. Becoming a bear snack was *not* how he'd planned to end his life. He looked up at the tree branches . . . way up . . . way, *way* up. Then again, falling off of a tree branch didn't seem like such a great ending, either.

Now that they'd been mentioned, bears became the hot topic in camp. Big Phil nudged Dad, who was unrolling his sleeping bag. "Remember that fellow back at the town where we gassed up the Jeep?"

"The Paiute Indian?" Dad responded. "Quite a character."

"He says a giant, man-eating grizzly roams these woods." Big Phil looked about to see if anyone was listening. They were. Funny how the term "man-eating" could prick up people's ears. Well, now that he had an audience . . . Big Phil's voice grew more dramatic. "The Paiute called him 'the Wild Bear of Giant Mountain!'"

"Come on, Phil," Dad said, "the Indian was just having some fun with you. If there are any bears around here at all, they're only small black ones."

"I wouldn't be so sure." Big Phil chuckled as he glanced around at the others who were listening with varying degrees of growing unease.

"Great!" Renee muttered to herself. "If I don't fall

off of a mountain, I'll be eaten by a bear." Suddenly she felt her dad's arm around her.

"You know, sweetheart, part of growing up is not believing everything you hear."

Renee gave him a look and sighed. OK, so being eaten by a bear had its pluses. At least it would stop the nonstop lecture series.

"In junior high," he droned on, "you'll hear all sorts of things. And you'll have to learn to use good judgment."

"That's if I *live* to see junior high," she replied.

Meanwhile Dad Martin had finished setting up his gear and strolled over for a friendly chat with Connie. "Hmmmm! What's for dinner?" he asked as he peered into the pot that was hanging over the fire.

Connie lifted a lid. "Dehydrated macaroni and cheese," she said. "I hydrated it myself."

"Hmmmm," Dad replied. He took a sniff—then fought back a slight gag. He glanced at Connie, who was smiling at him, waiting for a response. "Um . . . it smells really, really . . . hot," his voice trailed off, and he forced a smile.

"Thanks," Connie said with a good-natured grin, totally underwhelmed by his feeble attempt at a compliment. "Listen, could you watch these for a minute? I've got to help Giff." With that she handed the spoon to Dad and was off.

A moment later, Big Phil peered over Dad's shoulder. It had been fifteen minutes since he had pulled a joke on anyone, and he was starting to go through withdrawal. He reached down and looked under the lids of the other pots and pans—and his eyes lit up. Now *here* was a perfect opportunity.

"Hope you're hungry," he said to Dad.

"Sure am. But what's she got in there?" Dad was lifting a spoonful of the mixture out of a pan and eyeing it suspiciously.

"Oh, just the usual mountain fare," Big Phil answered casually. "Broiled rattler, squirrel sausage, stuffed owl . . ."

Suddenly Dad wasn't quite so hungry.

"He's never going to fall for that," Little Philip said from behind his dad. "He knows it's really hamburger and chicken."

Big Phil broke into another laugh and gave his boy a chuck on the chin. "My son doesn't always like my practical jokes."

"I wonder why," Dad mumbled under his breath.

In spite of the jokes about the food, everyone seemed to get through the meal without making any unscheduled trips into the bushes. And, for dessert, Big Phil pulled some candy from his pack and offered one to Dad. "Want a sugarless candy?"

Dad gave them a doubtful look and shook his head. "No, thanks, you go ahead."

Big Phil shrugged, popped a couple of candies into his mouth, then stood up and stretched. "I think I'll just visit the restroom. Or should I say the '*wildernessroom*'?" he said with a loud cackle.

On the other side of the campfire, Nicholas and Philip stared blankly into the flames. "I don't know about this Giant thing," Nicholas said softly, sitting with his back against a tall pine tree. "I mean, you risk your life . . . for what? Just to say you risked your life?" He shrugged. "I'm a cartoonist, not a rock climber."

Philip pushed his glasses back up on his nose and said in little more than a whisper, "Nick, I know I'm scared about most things. But this Giant *really* scares me."

"Me, too," mumbled Nick. "I hope our dads know what they're doing."

Nearby, Renee was still staring at her food, wondering if it would kill her. Suddenly she heard a rustling in the bushes. She glanced at Nick. "Did you hear something?"

The rustling grew louder.

Everyone froze.

Now they could hear heavy breathing.

Then there was a low, rumbling, growl.

That was it for Renee. She leaped to her feet and screamed, "It's the Wild Bear of Giant Mountain!"

Nick rose, trying his best to be cool and brave. Of course, he would have been more convincing if his knees weren't banging so loudly into each other. Still, somehow, he held his ground. "OK," he said nervously. "Ah, if it's a bear, he smells the food and . . . uh . . . probably just wants to . . . investigate."

"P-p-p-probably?" Philip stammered, rising and taking a step or two behind Nick.

Suddenly the loud rustling came from the other side of them. The children whirled around, but they were too late. A giant hairy paw reached out and grabbed Philip's leg.

The boy screamed, but it did no good. The paw

began pulling him into the bushes. Nick stood frozen in terror. Somewhere in the recesses of his brain he knew that someone had to act and act fast, or Philip would become the late-night munchie for some bear! But Nick's body wouldn't obey any of his commands to move.

"Help me!" Philip screamed. "Somebody help—"

Then, to everyone's amazement, the bear began to laugh.

"Hey! Wait a minute!" Renee cried. She took a step closer to the bear paw. "That's not a bear!" she yelled.

The laughter grew louder, and at last the bear paw released Philip. The three kids watched as, lo and behold, who should appear from out of the bushes but—you guessed it—Big Phil. He was covered with a blanket and laughing like he had never laughed before.

"No—*Har! Har! Har!*—it's not a—*Ho! Ho! Ho!*—Giant Bear. It's a giant—*Hee! Hee! Hee!*—slipper!" He continued laughing, holding up the bear-paw slipper. "Har-har-ho-ho-hee-hee! Boy, you guys were hysterical!"

Big Phil was so pleased with himself that he neglected to notice that no one else was laughing. Least of all poor Little Philip. There was no glee on his face. There wasn't any room for it with all the embarrassment and pain that was there. As Big Phil walked away, still laughing and congratulating himself on such a fine joke, Nicholas crossed over to Philip.

"You OK?" he asked.

The little guy tried to smile, but it was impossible to hide the tears filling his eyes. "No," he said hoarsely, "I'm not."

Nick was just as angry and embarrassed as Philip, but he felt bad for Philip and wanted to say something to cheer him up. "Hey, don't worry about it. Your dad was just trying to be funny."

"Yeah," Philip said, his voice thick with emotion, the tears starting to escape his eyes, trickling down his face. "But he never is." With that, Philip turned and headed toward his sleeping bag.

Nick ached for the guy, but he knew there was nothing he could do—at least for now.

FOUR
Facing the Giant

Sunrise in the mountains . . . What a sight. What an experience.

"What a pain," Nick groaned as he helped Renee hoist her pack onto her back.

Philip agreed. "When you're not climbing rocks, you're sleeping on them." He winced and rubbed his shoulder. "I'm even dreaming about rocks."

"I think Connie's boiling some for lunch," Renee grunted as she readjusted the straps around her waist.

At that moment, Dad Martin emerged from the trees. He was whistling a cheerful tune. Well, to him it was cheerful. To the kids it was torture. How could anyone be so happy so early?

"Hi, guys," he said and grinned. "I've been catching a few sunrise shots with my camera."

The kids mumbled something about "Give me a break," but Dad Martin didn't take the hint. He continued to hover, just as cheery as ever. "Well, today's the big day. Everybody ready to tackle the Giant?"

Nick sucked in his breath. For a moment he'd almost forgotten, but Dad was right. Today was the day. Today was the day they were going to climb that monster mountain.

Today was the day he was going to die.

Several minutes later they all were making their way down the trail. Birds sang. The sky glistened. It was a great day—unless you were wondering what it would be like to enter junior high on crutches.

"Tell me again," Philip muttered, "why are we putting ourselves through this?"

"I don't know," Nick answered. "All I can think about is that kids' book I used to read to my little sister. You know, *The Little Engine that Could?* Only this time I keep saying, 'I think I *can't,* I think I *can't,* I think I *can't.*'"

At last the group rounded the final turn and there it was. The Giant. A sheer rock face so high it put a crick in your neck just to look at it.

"We must've taken a wrong turn somewhere," Philip groaned, shoving up his glasses for what he was sure to be the very last time. Ever.

"We sure did take a wrong turn," Renee sighed, "back in Eastfield."

Nick wanted to throw in some clever comment, but his heart was so far up in his throat that it left no room for his voice.

"OK, everybody," Giff said as he began stringing the ropes and climbing equipment together. "The only way out of here is up and over."

So. This was it. The end to three promising young lives. The world would never know what it had missed: one rocket scientist, one lawyer (or was it hairdresser, she wasn't sure yet), and one great cartoonist . . . all snuffed out in their prime by a stupid pile of rocks!

Minutes later everyone was roped together as Connie gave last minute instructions on the climb: "Now remember, when you're halfway up, lean back on your rope so you can see that it's safe and feel more secure about trusting it."

Secure? Nick thought. *No way. How can you feel secure when you're dangling on the side of a cliff a million miles above ground? Besides, if God had meant for man to climb cliffs, he would have created him with goat's feet or suction-cup toes or little Spiderman tubes in his wrist for shooting out sticky webs.*

"Most important," Connie continued, "take your time, always check for good footholds." She turned to Giff and gave a nod. "OK, let's do it!"

In a flash, Giff took off up the rock face. It was like he'd climbed it a million times. Yeah, well, maybe he had. The guy *was* a pro. So no wonder it was so easy for him. Everyone watched as he worked his way up higher and higher.

"That doesn't look so hard," Renee said as she watched.

"I heard he was raised by a pack of mountain goats," Nick cracked.

At last Giff scrambled over the top, then looked down and gave a wave.

"OK." Connie turned to the group. "Who's next?"

Dead silence. Everyone stared at the ground. It was like being back in school. Everyone knew that if you let your eyes meet your teacher's you were dead meat. Everyone but Big Phil. Suddenly he stepped forward. "I'll go."

He took the rope in his hand and approached the cliff.

Philip watched in stunned amazement.

Connie helped the man connect his harness.

"Well, here goes nothing," Big Phil quipped and then, with a little hop, he was on the side of the rock and moving up.

"All right, Phil!" Dad Martin shouted.

Others clapped and cheered him on as he slowly made his way up the cliff.

"Be careful, Dad!" Philip cried. "Be careful!"

"No sweat," the man called over his shoulder. He continued looking for footholds as he slowly worked his way up the rock. Higher and higher and higher. Philip watched, growing more and more nervous.

At last the big man reached the top and, with Giff's help, he pulled himself over the ledge. The crowd below broke into applause. Big Phil looked back down and waved. He was breathing hard but he was all smiles. "Hello-o-o-o dow-ow-ow-ow-n the-e-e-e-e-e-ere!" he called.

It was over. Big Phil was safe. Philip could relax now. He could start breathing again. Then Connie turned to him and said, "How about following your dad?"

So much for breathing.

"I, uh . . . I don't, uh . . . that is to say . . ."

"Come on, Son," Big Phil called from above. "It's great!"

After a lot more coaxing and pleading, somehow Little Philip found himself stepping forward. He allowed Connie to help him with his harness.

Nick looked on with sympathy, wondering who the bullies at school would have to pick on when Philip wasn't around. Philip was probably wondering the same thing, but after a huge swallow and about a dozen deep breaths, he started up.

"All right, Philip!" the group cheered. "That-a-boy!"

"Way to go, Son!" Big Phil called from above.

Nicholas watched in amazement as the little guy inched his way up the wall. Philip was scared, there was no doubt about that, but he kept going and going and going. Finally he reached the ledge, and his dad pulled him over the top.

It was incredible. Everyone clapped and cheered and hollered.

"Yes!" Philip shouted as he rose to his feet. He stood beside his dad with his arms raised high. "YES!!"

"OK." Connie beamed with approval as she turned back to the crowd. "Who's next?"

"Let me give that a try," Dad Martin said as he stepped forward.

Nick was pretty nervous watching his father start up the rock, but after a couple of slips Dad began to get the hang of it. He had to stop a couple of times to catch his breath, but at last he reached the ledge and was hauled up to join Big and Little Phil at the top.

"Woooo!" he shouted. "That was terrific!"

Next came Renee. She was better than all the others. She scampered up the rock like a pro. Then came her dad. He was pretty good, too.

Finally the only ones left at the base of the cliff were Connie . . . and Nick. He looked up and swallowed hard. The only problem was that there was nothing left to swallow. His mouth was as dry as Death Valley.

"C'mon, Nick!" Dad shouted. "You can do it!!"

The boy tried to smile. There were Renee, her dad, Philip, Big Phil, and Dad all grinning down at him. Well, it was now or never. (And if Nick was honest, he had to admit that "never" sounded awfully good.)

He took a deep breath and stepped to the wall.

"That-a-boy," Connie encouraged him as she clipped in his rope. "Don't think about climbing the whole cliff. Just concentrate on one step at a time."

Nick nodded and looked for his first foothold—the same one all the others had used. Then he found the next one.

"That's good, Nick," Connie said. "Keep it up."

And he found the next.

And the next.

"Atta boy, Nicholas!" Philip shouted. "You're doing it, you're doing it!"

Slowly, step-by-step, Nicholas made his way up the wall. And slowly, step-by-step, his confidence grew. So this is what it felt like. Sure, he was getting a little tired, but the feeling that he was really accomplishing something pushed him on. Higher and higher.

Now he was half way up.

One step at a time, he kept thinking. *One step at a time.*

Then it happened. His foot slipped. When it did, his right foothold gave way. Nick tried to hang on with his hands, but it did no good. He'd lost his balance. Everything went into slow motion as Nicholas slipped away, fell from the wall, and tumbled toward the ground below.

"AUGGHHHHH!"

He thought he heard somebody scream but he wasn't sure. It might have been him. Then, at the very last second, he felt the safety rope jerk tight. It brought him up short and knocked the breath out of him, but it held him secure. That was the good news. The bad news was that he was dangling between heaven and earth—fifty feet above the ground. This was *not* his idea of a safe place. He began to panic.

"Help me! Get me down from here! SOMEBODY HELP ME!!"

"Nicholas!" Dad cried. "Nicholas! Look up here!"

But Nicholas couldn't. He couldn't take his eyes from the jagged rocks below.

"Get me down from here! Somebody get me down!"

"You're OK!" Giff called from above.

"Get me down!"

"It was just some loose rock," Giff continued. "Go ahead, find your footholds."

But Nicholas was too scared to find anything. He

just clung to the safety rope, white fisted, staring at the ground and shouting:

"Get me down! Get me down! GET ME DOWN!"

When I saw my buddy slip and slide down that rotten rock face, I knew—as only an all-knowing, all-courageous cartoon hero could know—that there was only one thing to do: Scream!

"GET HIM OFFA THERE! HURRY UP! SOMEBODY GET MOVING! HE'S GONNA DIE!!!"

Unfortunately, since Nick is the only one in the world who can hear me, the screaming wasn't a whole lot of help. So, with great derring-do—and a little derring-don't—I grabbed a harness, hooked onto the safety rope, and jumped.

OK, so it wasn't the brightest thing to do—but hey, my buddy needed me!

When I reached him, I hopped over close to his face and gave him my best so-brilliantly-white-that-you-gotta-be-encouraged-by-this smile.

"Come on, Nick," I said. "You can do it."

But when he opened his eyes just long enough to look at me, I saw something I'd never seen in my pal's eyes before. Total, complete, unrestrained terror.

Uh-oh.

In an instant Giff was over the side of the cliff and down the wall. He stopped beside Nick. "Hey, Nick, I'm right here, Pal. I'm right here."

Nicholas couldn't find his breath. He was still panicking and gasping for air.

"Don't worry, buddy, I'm right here."

"Just . . ." Nick tried to get control and to stop the panic. "Just get me down, Giff."

"No sweat, buddy," Giff's voice was low and soothing. "Just listen to me, and we'll go down together, OK?"

Nick nodded as he continued gasping for air.

"Now relax . . . don't look down and just relax . . ."

But Nicholas kept staring at the ground. He couldn't help himself.

"Stop it, Nick!" Giff spoke firmly, but softly. "Don't look down. Look up—look up!"

At last Nicholas obeyed. He tilted his head up. There above him were Dad, Renee, Philip, and Big Phil.

"You're OK, Son," Dad called. "Everything's OK."

Dad's voice and the familiar faces did the trick. Slowly a calm started to settle over Nick.

"Atta boy," Giff encouraged. "You just had a little slip, it happens to the best of us."

Nick nodded.

"Now get a handhold, and let's go down together."

Again Nick followed orders. He reached out to grab a nearby rock and pulled himself back to the cliff. Then slowly, ever so slowly, he copied Giff's movements and made his way to the ground.

At last Connie was able to reach up and ease him down the last few feet. "Not a bad first try, Nick," she said encouragingly.

Nick wasn't buying it. He had embarrassed himself beyond belief. He knew it. And he knew everybody knew he knew it.

Connie went on. "Next time you'll just have to—"

"Forget it!" he shouted, throwing off the harness. "There's not going to be a next time!"

Without another word, he stalked away into the woods.

FIVE

The Little Dentist Who Cried Wolf

Several minutes after Nick ran away from the Giant, he sat alone atop a boulder.

Too bad. He'd really been looking forward to junior high. Now it was definitely out of the picture. After what he'd pulled at the cliff, he'd be the laughingstock of the entire class. Make that the entire school!

It wasn't totally hopeless, though. He could still move into the basement. Mom could drop his food down the laundry chute. Nobody would even notice he was alive. Of course, that would make things like getting his driver's license, graduating from high school, going to college, and getting married a little tough, but he could get used to it.

Nicholas's pity party was in full swing when he spotted Giff approaching. *Oh no,* Nick thought, *now it's time for the ol' pep talk.*

Sure enough, Giff strolled up and plopped right down beside him. But to Nick's surprise the man said nothing.

Nicholas waited.

Still nothing.

Pretty soon the silence started to eat at him. What was this guy doing, anyway? Was he just going to go on sitting beside him saying nothing? Nick couldn't take it anymore. He blurted out, "I'm not going back!"

Giff's answer was quiet and calm. "Nobody's going to make you. That's your decision. I just want you to have all the facts before you decide."

"What facts?" Nick said scornfully. "That I'm a coward? That I'm scared of a little cliff?"

"You *should* be scared."

Nick looked at him.

"If you weren't, there'd be something wrong with you," Giff continued. "But you have to understand that, with the right equipment, it's perfectly safe."

"You call what happened out there *safe?*"

Giff grinned. "I haven't lost a camper yet."

Nick wasn't falling for it. "Why bother with all this anyway? Just to climb up some dumb rock?"

"Believe it or not, it's *fun*, Nick. You have a great sense of accomplishment, it's challenging . . . you make great friends."

"So far, you could say the same thing about baseball," Nick argued.

Giff broke into an easy smile. Nicholas had him there. "OK, how about this . . ." He hesitated a moment. Nick turned to him and waited.

"Climbing reminds us of how much we need God's help. He'll take us up any mountain, maybe one step at a time, but he'll get us there."

Nicholas's glance fell back to the ground.

"Remember, God made all this." Giff motioned toward the majestic mountains before them. "What better place to learn of his power and faithfulness than in the beauty of his creation?"

Nick looked up. It was true. The mountains before them were awesome. Come to think of it, so were the trees, the streams, the giant boulders, even that terrible Giant thing. And if God was powerful enough to create all of this then maybe, like Giff said, he might be powerful enough to be trusted.

At last Giff gave Nick a gentle slap on the back. "Come on," he said as he rose to his feet. "What say you and I squeeze in a lesson or two and tackle that cliff again tomorrow?"

"Lessons?" Nick asked.

"Sure, let's topple a couple of smaller giants before we go for the big guy."

The rest of that afternoon Nick and Giff worked out—tying knots, rappeling down cliffs, and learning other little tricks about not getting smashed to smithereens.

By supper time, Nicholas had it down. He was ready to fight the Giant again. Now there was just one little problem left.

What was he supposed to do with all his fear? Would he be able to handle it? Would he be able to keep it in control? There was only one way to find out.

Tomorrow he would have to face those fears head on.

Meanwhile, outside of camp, someone else was about to face a little fear. . . .

Big Phil was a couple hundred yards away from camp, gathering firewood. Because it was getting dark, and because he wasn't the most coordinated of campers, his foot caught on a log, and he fell flat on his face. Firewood flew in all directions.

"Great," Phil grumbled. He crawled to his feet and shook the dirt from his shirt. As a reward for his wonderful coordination (he rewarded himself for everything) he pulled a piece of sugarless candy from his fanny pack and popped it into his mouth.

He bent over and started picking up the wood, when suddenly, he heard a sound in the bushes behind him. Slowly he turned and peered into the undergrowth.

Something was rustling.

For the briefest second he panicked. Then, realizing what it was, he broke into a grin and shook his head. "C'mon, guys," he said as he bent back over to pick up the wood. "I know what you're trying to do, but it won't work."

More rustling.

"Cut it out now."

But they didn't cut it out. The rustling grew even louder.

"Oooo," Big Phil chuckled, "you got me real scared." He shook his head and muttered, "Amateurs," then started whistling as he picked up the last log and headed down the path.

The noise followed. Only now something else was added . . . breathing. Deep, heavy breathing.

Phil wasn't about to be fooled. After all, this was *his* joke; he'd started the game. "If you guys think

I'm gonna fall for that old trick," he laughed, "you gotta—"

That was as far as he got. His laugh stopped. His wood fell. He froze in his tracks. For suddenly, staring him directly in the face was . . .

"A-a . . . a ba-ba . . ." Big Phil tried to scream out the word, but not much was coming.

"Aaaaaaaa . . ." His mouth kept opening and closing, but he couldn't get out anything that sounded like a word.

"Aaaaaaaaaaaaaa . . . *BE-E-A-A-RRRRR!!"*

The huge grizzly bear slowly rose up on his hind legs. He towered several feet over Big Phil, who suddenly didn't seem so big anymore. The animal's huge nose jutted out at Phil, who, for a moment, wasn't sure if the bear was going to kiss his face or eat it. But it did neither. Instead it gave the man one long and loud sniff.

Phil remained frozen.

Slowly the beast lowered it's nose down to Phil's neck. It sniffed again.

Phil didn't move a muscle. He wasn't sure he could even if he had to.

Next the animal dropped its nose to his armpits and started sniffing again—and then it gave a violent sneeze. Suddenly Phil wished he'd used a little more deodorant.

"G-g-good b-b-bear . . . ," he stammered. "N-n-nice b-b-bear."

The bear paid no attention. It dropped its nose to Phil's waist and began sniffing his fanny pack. It moved no further. It just stayed there sniffing and snorting away.

At last Phil figured out what was happening. The bear wasn't after him, it was after his candy!

"Smell the c-c-candy, b-b-boy?" he asked.

In reply the soggy nose nuzzled the fanny pack harder.

Phil's mind raced. What could he do? There was only one choice. Slowly, ever so slowly he lowered his shaking hand down to the buckle.

The bear gave a little grunt.

Phil froze.

Then, after a minute, he started to unbuckle the pack. "Here-here you go, f-f-fellow . . . t-t-take the whole thing."

It seemed to take hours, but at last Phil freed the buckle and swung the pack toward the bear. "Good bear . . . eat the candy, now . . . eat the candy."

In response the bear exploded in a loud . . .

R O A R!

Phil screamed back. He couldn't help himself. For a moment it looked like the two were having a bellowing contest, but Phil didn't stick around to see who won. In a flash he turned and ran for his life . . . screaming all the way.

And that's how he entered the camp.

Screaming.

"AHHHHHHHH!!!"

Everyone looked up startled.

"A BEAR!!! IT'S THE WILD BEAR OF GIANT MOUNTAIN. HE ATTACKED ME!!"

Slowly, one by one, the group rolled their eyes.

Renee's father was the first to speak. "Right, Phil, we already heard that one."

"No! Really! In the woods, just past that big ridge . . . I was getting firewood . . . there was a giant Grizzly! Ten feet tall!"

Everyone began snickering.

"Phil, you got to get this straight," Dad Martin chuckled. "The wild bear of Giant Mountain is supposed to be a *black* bear, not a grizzly."

"No, no!" Phil insisted. "This was HIM! He ate my fanny pack!"

Everyone broke into laughter. The idea of a bear eating someone's fanny pack was too much.

"Maybe it was Yogi Bear," Renee's dad said. "Didn't he eat Mr. Ranger's pack once?"

The laughing grew louder.

Little Philip covered his eyes in embarrassment.

Big Phil was getting desperate. "You guys gotta believe me!! He was huge . . . brown . . . he wanted my sugarless candy!!"

By now everyone was in stitches. "Well, at least," Dad Martin said, laughing so hard he could barely squeeze out the words, "you're promoting good dental hygiene among bears!"

Everyone roared.

Everyone but Big Phil. The poor guy slumped down on a log. It was no use. He threw a look over to his son, but Philip was doing everything he could to look the other way. He was too embarrassed to even acknowledge his father was alive.

After dinner and a few more rounds of laughter over Big Phil's story, Giff rose and made an announcement. "Gather 'round, everybody."

Everyone turned to see what was up.

"Since this is our last night together, and since a part of this program is for fathers and children to grow closer to each other, we're going to do something a little different."

Everyone exchanged glances.

"After dinner," Giff continued, "we'll lead each family to your own camping spot for the night. You'll have a chance to share some time alone together and really communicate."

There was no missing the group's uneasiness. Both kids and grown-ups shifted as though the ground had just gotten a lot harder. Sure, this was what the kids and parents were *supposed* to do. But . . . a whole evening . . . together? A whole evening without TV, without going to the mall, without homework? Just talk? One-on-one? Heart-to-heart? Just dad and kid?

"Don't be afraid to be open with each other," Connie continued. "The idea is to spend some honest time communicating with one another."

The group threw sidelong glances at each other. Open? Honest? Communicating? Suddenly each father and matching kid began to wonder what, if anything, they really had in common.

"Giff and I will pick you up at 7:30 tomorrow morning," Connie concluded.

"But what about the Wild Bear?" Big Phil asked insistently.

"Phil," Giff said with a tolerant smile, "a joke's a joke, but let's concentrate on some *honest time* with Philip, OK?"

Big Phil's face drooped. "No one believes me!" he muttered in amazement. "No one."

SIX

One-on-One

An hour later each father-and-kid team had settled into their camping site for the night. No one was thrilled about this idea of just talking, but no one wanted to admit it.

Over in Renee's camp, "honest time" was taking the form of another one-man lecture. And since there was only one man in their camp, it was no real surprise who that lecturer was.

"And don't start wearing makeup too soon, either," Renee's dad warned. "Once you start with that stuff, you never go back."

Renee was doing her best to be patient. The best she figured, her dad had been going nonstop for nearly an hour. She was beginning to wonder if he'd taken time to breathe.

"Oh, and dating," he continued. "I know you're a teenager now, but no dating until you're at least . . . eighteen."

"Dad!" Renee cried.

"Seventeen?" he countered.

In another part of the forest, Big Phil and Little Philip sat side by side, throwing rocks into a lake.

"Bears don't like water, do they?" Big Phil asked, looking nervously over his shoulder. Actually, for the past hour, he'd spent a lot of time looking over his shoulder.

"Only if they're into waterskiing," Philip smirked.

"Not you, too!" Big Phil sighed. "*You* at least believe me, don't you?"

Philip gave him a long look. He still couldn't figure out if his dad was telling the truth or not. After all, the man had spent his entire life pulling practical jokes. Still, Giff had said this was the time for honesty . . . so Philip decided he might as well give it to his dad straight. "I just keep thinking that as soon as I believe you, you're going to say *'gotcha'* and start laughing at me."

"Son, I'd never laugh at—"

"Sure you do, Dad," Philip interrupted, looking his father square in the eye. "You do it all the time."

Now it was Phil's turn to look—really look—at his son. There was no trace of laughter or kidding on the boy's face. "Really?" Big Phil asked.

Philip nodded. "It makes me feel so stupid and, well . . ."

That was as far as the boy could get before the tears started welling up in his eyes. Big Phil looked on. When he finally spoke his voice was thick with emotion. "I guess that's something we gotta work on. . . ."

Little Philip brushed the moisture from his cheeks and nodded again.

They both sat there, silent, side by side, for the longest time.

Finally Big Phil cleared his voice. "I *really did* see a bear . . . *really!*"

Dad Martin entered the clearing where he and Nick had set up camp. Seeing Nick sitting on a boulder, silhouetted against the setting sun, he quickly snapped a picture.

Nick flinched with surprise. He'd been lost in thought. Tomorrow he was going to have to face the Giant again. And even with all the practicing he'd been doing with Giff, he still had a lifelong supply of fears stocked up. There were visions of the rope breaking, of the clamps giving way, and of falling fifty feet and taking a short cut to heaven. . . .

Dad replaced the lens cover and moved to sit next to his son. They looked out over the valley below. The sun was dipping into the mist atop the mountains; the light played in the clefts of the rock and on the sparkling ribbon of a winding stream below.

After a long moment, Dad finally spoke. "You know those ropes they have in gym class? The ones that go from the ceiling to the floor?"

"Yeah," Nick answered softly.

"Did I ever tell you about the time I was in junior high, and I raced my best friend Jerry Pedinkski to the top?"

"No. Did you win?"

"Well, sort of." Dad fidgeted slightly. "I'd never

climbed the ropes before. But somehow I beat Jerry to the top. That was the easy part."

Nicholas looked at his dad curiously.

"The hard part came when I looked down. Suddenly, I realized how far up I was."

"What did you do?"

"I panicked. I didn't know whether to slide or jump or just fall."

"What happened?"

"I remembered what one of the first guys that climbed Mount Everest said. He told someone he would never look down before he looked up. So, I looked up and prayed for help. Then I let myself down, hand over hand, one inch at a time. Ever since, whenever I start to look down, I look up first."

Nick took a deep breath and slowly let it out. "Every time I look up, all I see is the Giant."

"Well, pal, don't worry," Dad said, putting his arm around him. "I'm going to love you whether or not you climb another rock in your life."

"I've got the rocks figured out," Nick said with a wry laugh. "It's the mountain I'm worried about!"

They both laughed, and Nick's dad gave him a firm hug.

"Just remember, Son. Whether it's the mountain, or school, or any decision you'll have to make in life, everything you face takes courage."

Nick gave a nod.

"And you know where to look for that courage, right?"

Nick broke into a smile. "Just look up."

A few hours later, Nicky boy was in his sleeping bag cutting some ZZZZs . . . big time. I suppose the boy blunder had a right to doze. After all, it'd been quite a trying day for him.

But not for me. No-siree-bob. I'd spent the whole time cooped up in the sketch pad with nothing to do except ride in the Kentucky Derby, win the Olympic Downhill Slalom, and test-fly a few Navy jet fighters (it's kind of a big sketch pad).

With so little going on you can see why I had to break the monotony. I hopped out of the sketch pad and into Nicky boy's dreams (something you kids shouldn't try at home—unless, of course, you happen to be an imaginary character starring in your own home video and book series).

Suddenly I was standing at the bottom of the Giant—just me, my climbing gear, and my ballet shoes and tutu.

Ballet shoes and tutu!! Come on, Nick! You can dream better than that!

Poof! I was back in my Swiss yodeling outfit and Mexican sombrero.

Mexican sombrero!?

Poof! No sombrero. (I tell you, it ain't easy living in a kid's imagination.)

Now, where were we? Oh yeah. I began swinging the rope with its grappling hook around and around my head. With a marvelously macho and manly toss I flung the hook to the top of the cliff, where it grabbed hold beautifully.

Well, almost beautifully. The fact that it landed in the middle of an eagle's nest was a little problem. And the fact that when I yanked on the rope I pulled the nest and eggs down on top of me was another problem. And if that wasn't enough, ol' Momma eagle decided to swoop down and give me a piece of her mind. Not that she had that much to share. I mean, she was, of course, a "bird brain."

When she finished shooting off at the beak, I tried again. Once again I threw the grappling hook perfectly. Once again it grabbed hold marvelously. Once again I tugged the rope to tighten it. And once again I dragged something over the edge.

Luckily, it wasn't another nest full of eggs. With my cholesterol I couldn't stand to have seconds. It was just a five hundred–ton boulder.

A FIVE HUNDRED–TON BOULDER?!!

Nicholas . . . Nicholas wake up! NICHOLAS!"

But Nick was still snoozing.

The boulder started falling toward me. I had to run away! I had to jump to the side! I had to call my life insurance agent to make sure my premiums were paid up.

Closer and closer it came . . .

I leaped to the left.

It bounced to the left.

I leaped to the right.

It bounced to the right.

No doubt about it, the boulder and I were about to become inseparable buddies. It was about to make one giant impression on me!

Finally, I had no place to go, unless I jumped off this page and into your lap (then we'd see how funny you think this all is!), but ol' Boulder Babe saved me the effort—(and you the pain)—she hit me dead center.

SPLATTT!

Talk about having a crush on someone.

You know, they say a rolling stone gathers no McGee, but don't you believe it. When I finally managed to push the bulging boulder off of me, I was flatter than a football tackled by a semi. Of course, that didn't stop me. No way. Nicholas had all night to dream . . . , which unfortunately meant I had all night to climb. So I began scaling that mountain with my bare hands.

Higher and higher I climbed. Pooped-er and pooped-er I became.

Things were getting a little tiresome when Momma Eagle decided to drop by for a little chit-chirp. She was still a little steamed about those eggs. So, pulling out a tail feather, she began to tickle me. I started to snicker. Then chuckle. Then chortle. Then guffaw. Then, before I could think of any more synonyms for "laugh," I turned to my feathered friend and shouted:

"Hey, this is no laughing matter!"

But she was all smiles—not an easy thing to do with a beak for a mouth. 'Cuz she knew what was coming. And what was coming was my hands . . . loose, that is. Yup, free, unattached, no longer fastened to anything. But air.

I had heard of dying with laughter, but this was ridiculous. I scrambled for another handhold, but it was no use. I fell off of that cliff face faster than a kid's smile melts after learning she has mumps on Halloween. The ground raced toward me, complete with all its sharp and probably very uncomfortable rocks.

Suddenly I had a brain squall. (It would have been a brainstorm, but I don't have that big of a brain.) I began flapping my arms. (Hey, don't blame me, it's not my dream.) Thanks to Nick's vivid imagination, it did the trick! Soon my flapping brought me to a stop. Sooner than that, I was soaring upward. And even sooner than that, I landed on top of the Giant.

Ahhhh, safe at last.

Well, not exactly . . .

It seems the Giant didn't exactly get his name by accident; he got it because he was a giant! That's right, a huge gigantic giant made out of living rock! And, at the moment, I was standing on his head!

"N I C H O L A S ! ! !"

Rock Head gave a blink. Then another. And another. Something was in his eye. Actually, it was me. I was in his eye. (Or is it "Eye was in his I"?) But this was no time for an English lesson. The point is, this was getting too dangerous (not to mention ridiculous). So I leaped from his eyelid and raced across the top of his nose. He snorted and huffed and puffed, but I was one allergy he couldn't get rid of.

I ran over to his ear and hopped in.

It was like a giant tunnel that went on forever. "Hello . . . ello . . . ello . . . ello. Can anybody hear me . . . hear me . . . hear me . . . ?"

But Rocky Boy wasn't in the mood to lend me his ear—or any other part of his body. He reached down and took hold of the nearest tree. To me, it was a huge pine. To him, it was about the size of a

Q-Tip. Raising the giant "Pine-tip" to his ear, he began pushing it inside.

Squeak-squeak-squeak-squeak!

Closer and closer the branches came toward me. Deeper and deeper I ran into the Giant's ear. Then, before I knew it, I came flying out of his other ear. Talk about being empty-headed! This guy was brainless . . . literally.

To prove it, he shoved the Pine-tip in so hard it came out the other side, too. Unfortunately, it snagged my climbing rope with one of its branches and, before I knew it, ol' Boulder Brain had wound my rope—and me—around and around the trunk.

"Put me down!" I shouted. "Put me down!"

Happy to oblige, he flipped me down like a yo-yo. Unfortunately, like any good little yo-yo, I came right back up.

Then back down.

Then back up.

Down and up. Down and up. I was feeling worse than the New York Stock Exchange until suddenly the rope broke and I went plummeting toward the earth.

Now, being the cool and collected thinker that I am, I did what made the most cool and collected sense. I screamed like a madman.

"N I C H O L A S!!! N I C H O L A S, W A K E U P!!!"

SEVEN
A New Day

Nick's eyes popped open. He hated it when McGee got into this dreams like that. He glanced around, trying to remember where he was. Oh yeah, the real campsite, in the real woods, in the real world. Once that was settled he sat up, rubbed his eyes, and looked at his watch.

"Ooouuu!" he cried. "Seven thirty . . . No way!"

He hopped to his feet, shook his head, and slapped his cheeks—anything to jolt himself totally awake. This was the big day—the day he'd tackle the Giant—and he figured it would be better to do it awake.

He looked over to where Dad was sleeping . . . but there was no Dad. Just his rolled-up sleeping bag.

That's weird, Nick thought. *Where could he be?*

Over at another campsite, Renee and her dad also were packing. Well, at least Renee was packing. Her dad was still on the lecture circuit. Rumor had it that the guy even lectured in his sleep. From the way Renee looked, it was a pretty good bet that the rumor was true.

"And don't ride with anyone who hasn't had their license for at least two years," he said. "Oh, and another thing, don't—"

Right there, with her dad's three hundred forty-second rendition of "and another thing," Renee decided enough was enough.

"Daddy!" she practically screamed. "Please! *Stop!*"

For a moment her dad was taken back by the outburst. But only for a moment.

"I know I'm going awfully fast," he admitted, "but I don't have a lot of time with you and—"

"Daddy!"

"I have so much I want you to remember, and—"

"DADDY!!"

At last she'd gotten through to him. He stopped talking. He looked a little surprised. Then a little sheepish.

Renee walked up and, without a word, gave him a giant-sized hug. He looked even more surprised. Finally, she spoke.

"Daddy, I'm going to remember this as the best vacation I ever had." She stopped the hug long enough to look up into his eyes. "And I'll remember that you love me a whole lot."

Taking her face into his hands, Ted nodded. "I love you with all my heart."

Renee could feel her throat tightening with emotion, and she did her best to blink back the tears. She smiled. "Just because I'm a teenager doesn't mean I'm going to forget everything you taught me while I was growing up."

Her dad wanted to interrupt, but he had the feeling he'd been doing enough of that lately. Instead, he kept silent and let her continue.

"Don't you see? You can stop telling me all the *don'ts,* because you spent ten years teaching me all the right *dos.*"

"It's . . . it's just so hard," he stuttered, "being so far away and wanting to be there to protect you."

"I know. I miss you, too," she said as she buried her face in his chest. Then, after a long moment she looked back up at him. "But the things you taught me as a kid keep coming back. I mean it's like you're still with me." She smiled again, and this time the tears started to spill over. "Well, almost . . ."

Now it was her dad's turn to blink back tears. He'd forgotten how fiercely he cherished his little girl. More importantly, he'd forgotten how proud he was of her. For a long moment the two stood in the woods, holding each other, softly crying. Not because of pain, or fear, or loss.

But because of love.

Over in the third campsite, Big Phil was packing up. And I do mean packing: throwing things in here, shoving things in there, all the time muttering to himself. The guy was definitely in *some kind of mood.*

"If those guys don't believe me," he grumbled, "I'm going to have to show 'em a thing or two. Just wait 'til I try the old crazed moose routine!"

Philip had had enough. Something inside him snapped. "Dad! Stop!"

The outburst brought the older man to a halt. Philip didn't want to hurt his dad's feelings, but he'd gone this far, so he'd better finish.

"Dad . . . everyone's tired of your jokes."

His father's eyes widened slightly. "But . . . son, they don't even believe me. I mean, I was nearly eaten by a bear and they don't—"

"Were you?" Philip demanded.

Again Big Phil stopped. He gave his son a long look. Slowly, the realization sank in. Not that nobody believed him . . . but *why* nobody believed him. "I guess I . . . uh . . . I cried wolf one too many times, huh?"

He kept looking at Philip, hoping the boy would argue, but for once in their lives they were in total agreement.

After a long moment Big Phil let out a heavy sigh. "Is there anything I can say that will make *you* believe me?"

Philip shrugged. "I don't know. I guess it's like Giff said, just be honest."

Big Phil took a deep breath. It had been a long time since he had tried that approach, but maybe it was worth a shot. "OK," he said, moving to sit beside his son. "I was so scared . . . I was so scared I could barely move. I kept thinking what it would be like never to see you or your mother or your sister again. I kept thinking there are so many things that I still had to tell you. I kept thinking . . ."

But that was enough honesty. Big Phil broke off and just stared at the ground.

"Go ahead," Little Phil urged. "You kept thinking what?"

Finally Big Phil looked up and continued. "I kept thinking how ironic it would be for Mr. Practical Joker to be eaten by a 'mythical' bear."

He tried to laugh, the way he always did when things got too serious, but Little Phil was not joining in. Instead, his son searched his father's face. Then he asked as honestly and sincerely as he knew how:

"So you really do love us?"

"Oh yeah, pal," Big Phil smiled as he brushed away the tears starting to fill his eyes. Jokes he could handle, but this honesty stuff was really tough. "I love . . ." He took a moment to swallow. "I love you more than you'll ever know."

Over at the Martin campsite, Nick had finished packing up the ropes and equipment. He looked around. Still no Dad. He checked his watch. It was getting late. This wasn't like his father. Not at all. Dad was never late to anything.

Then Nick spotted them. Dad's footprints. They headed away from the campsite and directly into the bushes. Nick's heart started to pound. A faint chill ran through his body as he began to wonder if maybe Big Phil was telling the truth. Maybe there really was a bear in the area.

He shook the thought off. Impossible. And yet Big Phil seemed so sure.

Just to be safe, Nick grabbed his dad's pack and hung it on a tree branch before turning and starting into the forest.

"Dad! Dad, where are you?!"

EIGHT
Nicholas vs. the Giant

Several minutes after Nick left the campsite, Giff arrived.

"Good morning!" he called. "Time to head back."

No one answered. And for a good reason: no one was there.

"David? . . . Nick?"

Then he spotted Dad Martin's backpack hanging in the tree. His forehead creased with the beginning of worry, and he searched the area around him more carefully. Finally he noticed the footprints, two pairs of them . . . both heading out into the bushes.

Giff grabbed the pack from the tree and started to follow—but very carefully.

Nick made his way through the woods, doing his best to be cautious. The last thing in the world he wanted was to be eaten by a bear . . . especially just before he started seventh grade. Picture it: all those years of suffering through childhood, all those years of waiting to reach teenagerism, and then, just when your voice has changed—

CRUNCH, GULP, BURP.

You become some overgrown carpet's snack.

No, thank you.

Soon, the cliff came into view—the one Nicholas and Dad had sat on to watch the sunset the night before. Of course! Why hadn't Nick thought of it? Dad had obviously come to get a few more photos.

"All right, Dad," Nick said as he pushed the last of the bushes aside, "we'd better get—" But the boy came to a stop. There was no one around.

"Dad. . . ."

No answer.

"Dad? Can you hear me? Daaaad!"

Ditto in the no-answer department.

Shaking his head, Nicholas turned to leave. Then he heard something—or he thought he did.

"What?" he called, "Did somebody—?"

He heard it again. It was a small cry:

"Help . . ."

He looked around.

"Help me. . . ."

It came from the cliff! Nick raced to its edge and peered over. "Dad?" He scanned the face of the cliff. For a moment he saw nothing. Just lots and lots of rock that seemed to stretch down forever. A wave of dizziness washed over Nicholas, but he forced himself to keep looking. Then he spotted him.

"Dad!"

He dropped to his knees. There, dozens of yards below, clinging to a small ledge, was his father.

Even at that distance there was no missing the gash across his forehead and his bloody arm.

"Nick . . ." Dad's voice was faint and weak. "Help me. . . ."

Nicholas's mind raced. What could he do? In a second the answer came. Nothing! His dad was too far away. He had to get somebody. "I'm going for help," he cried.

"I . . . can't hold on!" Dad gasped. A patch of rocks beneath his hand gave way, and Dad struggled for a better hold. More rocks gave way. It was clear: the ledge that kept him from tumbling down the cliff was crumbling to pieces by the second.

Nicholas panicked. Big time. If he ran for help, Dad would be at the bottom of the cliff when he got back. As though proving that point, more rocks slipped from under his father's grip.

"Nicholas . . ."

OK, OK . . . get hold of yourself, Nicholas thought. *There's got to be something I can do.*

He had it! Slipping the pack from his shoulders he called down, "Hold on, Dad!" He unzipped his pack and pulled out a rope. Dropping back to his stomach he carefully lowered it toward his father. It was a little scary being that close to the edge and hanging one arm over, but that was his dad down there.

At last the rope brushed against his father's shoulder.

"Just grab hold of the rope!" Nicholas shouted.

Dad nodded. But as he moved to reach for it even more rocks gave way. He started to slide.

"NICHOLAS!"

"DAD!"

Rocks tumbled and fell as the man continued to slide. Then somehow, miraculously, he got another handhold and came to a stop. He coughed and choked as dust blew up around him.

"Dad! Are you OK? Dad? *D A A A D!!*"

"Yeah . . . I'm fine," came the weak voice as Dad Martin coughed and choked some more. "But my arm . . . I can't move my arm. . . ."

Great, Nicholas thought. *Now what?*

He already knew the answer. There was no way Dad could pull himself up by the rope. Someone had to go down there and tie the rope around him. Since there was no one else around, Nick had a sneaking suspicion who that "someone" would have to be. He swallowed hard.

"Nicholas. . . ."

He bit his lip, feeling the panic start to swell up inside of him. Then he remembered his Dad's words from the night before: Never look down before looking up. Taking a deep breath, Nick looked up toward heaven.

"Please, God," he murmured, "please. . . ." It wasn't much of a prayer, but Nick knew the Lord knew what he meant. If ever he needed courage, it was now.

Quickly Nick moved to act. He pulled his harness from the backpack and slipped into it. "Hang on, Dad!" he shouted.

He looked around and found a good sturdy rock. Next he tied his rope around it, reciting Giff's instructions, "All the way twice . . . clamp . . . secure . . . double check . . . OK." He was breathing hard—like he'd run a hundred-yard dash. He knew that wasn't good. He'd have to control his breathing—and his fear—better than that.

Finally everything was set. It was now or never. Nick eased himself to the edge. Then, glancing up to heaven with another quick, "Please, Lord . . . ," he let out the rope and stepped backward over the edge. "Hang on, Dad, I'm coming!"

Carefully, step-by-step, Nick made his way down the cliff, searching for cracks, pounding in the small anchors that secured the rope. His breathing was still hard and fast but that was as much from the work as it was from the fear. Yet, the more he concentrated on the work the more the fear seemed to disappear.

Until one of his footholds gave way. An avalanche of rock and gravel cascaded down upon his father.

"Dad!" Nick yelled. "DAD!"

No answer.

"DAD?!!"

Finally he heard it. More coughing and choking. Then the familiar voice. "It's OK, Son . . . keep coming . . . everything's OK. . . ."

But it wasn't OK. Not at all. Dad's voice was growing weaker by the second.

Nick closed his eyes. He couldn't worry about that. He couldn't panic. He had to think of the job before him—nothing more. He had to plant those anchors securely into the rocks and carefully work his way down. One step at a time.

And so he continued. One step at a time. One

step at a time. It seemed to take forever, but finally . . . he was there.

"Dad!" The sight of his father made him gasp. There was a deep gash across the man's forehead, his shirt was torn, and blood was streaming down his arm. He had no climbing gear, just the camera dangling loosely around his neck.

"I . . . wanted a sunrise shot." Dad coughed. "I wasn't even that close to the edge. . . . It just gave way."

"Don't talk, Dad. Save your energy," Nick warned. "We're not out of this yet."

Since Dad couldn't use his arm, the two of them had to go up together. Quickly Nick fashioned a makeshift harness around Dad's waist.

A few more rocks slipped away.

"It looks like this whole ledge is about to give out," Nicholas warned.

Next he tied Dad's harness to his. More rocks fell. He had to work fast. Finally, he had it. When he was sure everything was good and secure Nick tried to grin. "What say we get out of here?"

Dad gave a nod—just as the worst possible thing happened.

The entire ledge gave way!

"AUGHHHHHH!" they yelled as the rocks crumbled and disappeared from under them.

Nick and his father began to fall, tumbling in midair—but only for a second. A moment later the rope pulled them up short.

"OOOAAAAF!"

It knocked the wind out of them, but they were safe! At least that's what Nick hoped. It took all of his courage to open his eyes—and then he wished he hadn't. They were dangling beside the cliff . . . in midair . . . hundreds of feet above the ground!

But the anchors were holding. If Nick hadn't taken the time to carefully secure them, the two of them wouldn't be dangling right now . . . they'd still be falling.

The boy hung there a minute, trying to catch his breath. He was breathing too hard and too fast again. *Please, God, help me to relax. Help me to trust you.*

Slowly, miraculously, his mind began to clear. Finally he had a plan.

"I'm going to climb up first," he said. "I'm going to clamp on to the anchors and then try to pull you up, OK?"

"OK," Dad Martin gasped.

With great effort Nick pulled them closer to the rocky wall. Then, slowly, he started making his way upward to the first anchor. It was excruciating work, pulling and helping his father along, but there was no other way.

At last they arrived at the anchor.

Then, pausing to catch their breath, they moved up to the next anchor, then the next, and the next. Nearly every step caused more rocks to slip and slide away.

Yet Nicholas continued. His arms and legs started to tremble and shake from exhaustion. Still he pushed upward.

"There's a handhold just above," he said to his dad.

Dad reached for it with his good arm.

"There! Good. Now—"

But his dad couldn't hang on. Even his good arm was too weak.

"Look out!"

More rocks crumbled and slid away.

Nick strained to pull his dad up, but his strength was nearly gone. He couldn't budge his father's dead weight.

Now what? Nick wondered frantically. Once again he looked up, toward heaven, for help. And once again there was an answer—this time in the form of a strong tug on the rope.

It was Giff! He stood above them on the cliff, the rope in his hand. "Hang on!" he shouted and began pulling them up.

Nick let out a weary sigh as they scooted up the cliff. They were going to be OK.

Giff reached down to grasp Dad Martin firmly, hoisting him over the edge of the cliff, onto solid ground. Nick wanted to kiss the ground, which he could have done easily since he was laying, face down, too tired to move. Instead, he looked at his dad. Their eyes met.

"You did it," Dad croaked. It wasn't just the dust and dirt that was choking his father. It was the pride he had in his son. "You did it!"

Slowly the realization sank in. Nick had beaten the unbeatable! It wasn't just that he had beat the Giant. It wasn't even that he had saved his father's life (though he figured that would sure come in handy when he wanted to borrow the car in a few years).

The point is, Nick had beaten the one thing he

had never thought he could take on, the one thing that had threatened to make him miserable for the rest of his life. Nick had beaten his fear—and that felt great!

NINE
Wrapping Up

"So that's the Giant?" Mom asked as she sat on the couch looking at the slides on the screen.

"That's it," Dad said. "'Course it looks a lot scarier in person than from this sofa."

The rest of the group agreed. They also agreed that it was great to be back home. Back to CD players, microwaves, and TVs with forty-seven channels. No more rising at the crack of dawn, no more dehydrated macaroni, no more carrying around your own toilet paper.

Civilization. Aahhh, the roar of the freeway, the smell of the exhaust, the . . . well, you get the picture.

Exactly one week (and a few hours) after Nick and Dad's little 9-1-1 adventure on the Giant, the whole group—except for Ted, Giff, and Connie—was gathered in the Martin family room, watching the slide show. Grandma, Jamie, and Sarah were there, too.

Dad clicked to another slide of the Giant.

"You climbed down *that* to save your father?" Mom asked in amazement.

Nicholas shrugged. "I didn't know it was the Giant at the time."

"It still makes you a hero," Dad insisted as he fumbled to change slide trays. Having one arm in a sling was slowing him down a little.

"That's right!" Big Phil shouted as he slapped Nick on the back. "The boy is a hero!"

Philip and Renee added their own cheers, as they pounded Nick on the back, rapped his head, and tousled his hair. Being a hero can be pretty painful.

There was other good news, too. Since Renee knew the whole story, it was just a matter of days before the whole world knew the whole story. And if the world knew, well, let's just say that maybe junior high wouldn't be so tough for Nick, after all.

Dad slipped in the slide tray and clicked to the next picture. It was a slide of Renee reaching the top of the Giant.

"Way to go, Renee!" Dad cheered. Everyone joined in as Renee enjoyed her own turn of back-slapping, head-rapping, and hair-tousling.

"I still can't believe it," Renee giggled. "I actually climbed a mountain!"

Next came the shot of Connie stirring a pot over the campfire. There were no choruses of glee here. Just lots of groans.

"What's she cooking?" Jamie asked.

"Broiled rattlesnake, squirrel sausage, and a side of poached porcupine," Philip quipped.

"Like father, like son," Big Phil whispered

proudly to Mom Martin. She chuckled, but the look on her face showed she was a little worried about Philip's future.

"I'm not falling for that old trick," Jamie shot back to Philip. "It was probably just a bunch of dehydrated junk."

Philip looked a little disappointed until his dad threw his arm around his shoulder. "Don't worry, son—developing a refined sense of humor just takes time."

Nick and Renee exchanged nervous glances. They obviously hoped it would take forever.

"Hey, speaking of food," Mom said, "I think you all deserve some more chips and dip!"

"No argument there!" Big Philip practically bellowed.

"No, Phil," she said forcing a smile, "somehow I didn't think there would be. Nicholas, you want to bring them in here?"

"Sure," Nick said as he rose and headed into the kitchen.

I would have been in the family room oohhing and ahhing over the slides, but since Mr. Dad didn't take any pictures of me (that's one of the disadvantages of being an imaginary character), I knew there wouldn't be much to ooh and ahh over.

But that's OK. I'd just discovered something much more exciting than a bunch of slides. I mean, forget the incredible scenery, forget the unbelievable mountains, forget the phantasmagorical sunsets. I'd discovered something more incredibly incredible than all of that.

I'd discovered my own reflection in the kitchen toaster!

Talk about a work of art! I'd forgotten how beautifully my biceps bulged, how tremendously my trapezoids tapered, how delicately my deltoids . . . er, uh . . . toided.

"McGee, what are you doing?" It was Nicholas.

"Just admiring the scenery," I answered as I struck another pose. But you can only take so much of a great thing, so finally I tore my eyes away from me. "So," I said, "when do you think we're hittin' the ol' Giant again?"

"I don't think I need to climb the Giant again," Nick said as he swooped into the cupboard and fridge for a little chips and dip raid.

"What? You think you're ready for Mount Everest, now?" I asked as I tossed my handy-dandy rope and grappling hook up to the top of the nearby aquarium.

"Naww. . . ." Nick shrugged. "But I've got a feeling there will be plenty of giants right here, every day."

"Giants?" I cried. "Here??" I quickly dashed around the aquarium for cover.

"No, McGee," Nick laughed. "What I mean is, courage isn't something you get it the wilderness. It's always here when you need it. God helps you find it."

"Oh, yeah, right," I chuckled as I stepped back out from behind the aquarium. "I knew that."

As a reward for my great courage, Nicholas took a cookie off of the plate and left it on the counter for me. "Here's one for the road," he said with a grin.

"The road?" I shouted. Quicker than you can say, "Now what's he up to?" I grabbed the rope and scampered to the top of the aquarium. After a quick change into my snorkel, flippers, and diving gear, I continued, "Next year, what say we hit the road and do scuba adventures with Mom?"

With that I gave a mighty leap into the tank. Luckily, Nick hadn't painted me with watercolors that day, or things could have gotten a little messy.

Nicholas watched as I dove neatly into the water. The goldfish all broke into applause and turned over their score cards revealing: "9.5," "9.4," "9.9," and "2.3." (Hey, you know how tough those Chinese judges can be.)

Still, I had no time to pick up my medal. I was too busy heading for the open oyster shell at the bottom. There, right before my baby blues, was a pearl bigger than any dustball ever discovered under Nicky's bed. It was time to do what I did best. It was time to risk life and limb for riches and greed.

I dove straight into ol' Pearly's mouth, when suddenly she thought it was time for a little McGee meal. Quicker than you can say, "This is going to hurt," she snapped her cast-iron lips around me.

"YEOWWW!" I screamed as bubbles bubbled around me. "Nicholas. . . ."

Blubble . . . blubble . . .

"Nicholas, get me . . ."

Blubble . . .

". . . out of here!!"

Of course, Nicholas showed his great compassion by breaking into a good case of the laughs.

"McGee!" he said, laughing and shaking his head.

But I wasn't worried. No-siree-bob. How could I be? I'm the hero of these stories . . . and real heroes never get killed—especially by toothless clams.

So stay tuned, scuba fans, as soon as I get out of this predicament I know there'll be another one just around the corner. Until then . . .

"Nicholas. Nicholas?"

Blubble . . . blubble . . .

"N I C H O L A S S S S . . . !"